Life is a series of changes. —*Anna Ciuni*

Published by Two Lions, New York • www.apub.com

Amazon, the Amazon logo, and Two Lions are trademarks of Amazon.com, Inc., or its affiliates.

ISBN-13: 9781542006200
ISBN-10: 1542006201

The illustrations were rendered digitally.
Book design by Abby Dening

Printed in China • First Edition

10 9 8 7 6 5 4 3 2 1

I AM JUST A PIECE OF PAPER—
orange with white and blue spots.
Then a boy folds me many times,
giving me a head, tail, and wings.

I am his Origami Crane,
and he is My Boy.

He keeps me on his nightstand.
I am the last thing he sees each night
and the first thing he sees each morning.

My Boy sails me around his room.

Dipping, diving,

dreaming.

Sometimes,
My Boy's eyes
fill with tears, and
he holds me close.
His heart goes
bump-da-bump
against my wings
    as he
        talks
            to me.

When shadows fill his room
and the house **squeaks** and **creaks**,
I protect My Boy.

On nights when the moon is bright

and stars sparkle in the sky,
together My Boy and I make wishes.

But over the years, My Boy talks less and less to me. The shadows don't scare him anymore. His picture books disappear. We stop making wishes.

I am dusty but still on his nightstand. And still the last thing he sees each night and the first thing he sees each morning.

One day, My Boy places
a photograph in front of me.
I peek around and see
a picture of a girl with
an orange, white, and
blue shirt. *My* colors,
I fume.

Now *she* is the last thing
he sees each night and
the first thing he sees
each morning.

Years pass, and My Boy finds me behind the photograph
and picks me up. My wings flutter, and I think we might
sail around the room once more, but instead he unfolds me.

I'm just a piece of paper again.
Orange with white and blue spots.

My Boy scrawls tickling words
across my surface
and folds me back up.

He takes me to the girl in the photo.
She unfolds me, and her tears make me
soft and damp.

"Yes, I will marry you," she says.

Now she is My Girl, too. My Boy folds me
back into Origami Crane.

On My Boy and Girl's nightstand, I am the last thing they see each night and the first thing they see each morning.

One day, My Boy picks me up. He makes other cranes
and hangs them from a wire, with me in the center.
He tells me they are my flock. The wire spins
and we soar. Not long after, My Boy and Girl
place a bundle of orange, white, and blue
beneath my flock. *My* colors, I think happily.

The bundle
giggles
and **gurgles**.
My Boy and Girl
smile tenderly.
And then
I realize—
it's a baby.

Our baby!

My flock and I are the last thing
Our Baby sees each night and
the first thing he sees each morning.

He is ours
and we are his,
and he loves us.

I realize now that I was never just
a piece of paper, orange with
white and blue spots.